blue
rider
press

THE BOOK OF MEMORY GAPS

Cecilia Ruiz

Blue Rider Press
a member of Penguin Group (USA)
New York

blue
rider
press

Published by the Penguin Group
Penguin Group (USA) LLC
375 Hudson Street
New York, New York 10014

USA • Canada • UK • Ireland • Australia
New Zealand • India • South Africa • China

penguin.com
A Penguin Random House Company

ISBN 978-0-399-17193-2

Printed in China
10 9 8 7 6 5 4 3 2 1

BOOK DESIGN BY CECILIA RUIZ

To Philip, and all the memories
we may forget

We are the things we don't remember,
the blank spaces, the forgotten words.

VALENTIN

Valentin does not remember how certain objects look,
thus he often mistakes one thing for another.
Lately, he has been carrying around all kinds of bouquets.
It appears the little boy is in love.

POLINA

After her fall, Polina was not able to create new memories.
She lived believing every night was the *opening night*.
The first of many tragedies was having to wear a used discolored costume.
The last, and most painful, was performing for an empty theater.

PAVEL

Pavel keeps forgetting what he just did.

He has been rehearsing the same melody over and over for almost a year.

The entire neighborhood has left.

VERONIKA

Veronika was bad at faces but good with smells.
She learned to make perfumes and gave them to the ones she loved
so she might know when they were near.

SIMON

Simon had a prodigious memory. He could remember, almost as if he had
committed them, every single act of sin ever confessed to him.
It was no longer strange to see him in the confessional room,
hoping to be purged of his borrowed sins.

KOKA

One morning Koka found a bag of useless money under the bed. She recalled it was her hidden stash, only this time the bills were no longer in circulation. Assaulted by feelings of embarrassment and self-torture, she spent the day making a list of all the things she would have done with the money.

PYOTR

Pyotr possessed the ability to repeat with accuracy what he had only heard once.
He enjoyed whistling from memory, especially on lonely days,
the song of a bird he had once heard.

IVAN

Ivan took the few things he owned and left. He found a quiet spot on the mountainside where he could smell the yellow vapors coming from the old factory. It was the same musty aroma that would drift from his grandfather's hat when Ivan rode on his shoulders as a child.

NADYA

Even though Nadya has never seen the ocean, she believes she remembers swimming in it. She vividly recalls its smell and the way the salt water made her eyes sting. She remembers an unfamiliar vastness she longs to feel again.

ALEXANDER

Alexander quit his career as a composer when, for the fifth time, without noticing it, he wrote a piece that already existed.

VIKTOR

Every evening, Viktor arrived home on the same shore, thinking that he had been at sea for months. His wife would be there to welcome him, though he had left that same morning.
Sadly for him, his wife's excitement could never equal his.

NATASHA

Natasha constantly has words on the tip of her tongue.
She keeps feeling she is about to remember, but they never come.
She spends her days searching for all of her missing words.

IGOR

Igor has never been able to get over the humiliation of a false memory.
He keeps recalling a fight that never took place. A tight battle he never lost.

LUCYA

The farthest Lucya was able to get out of her house was determined by the number of scarves she owned. She started mistrusting her memory two years before when, one afternoon, she was unable to find her way back home.

We are our memory,
we are that chimerical museum of shifting shapes,
that pile of broken mirrors.

JORGE LUIS BORGES

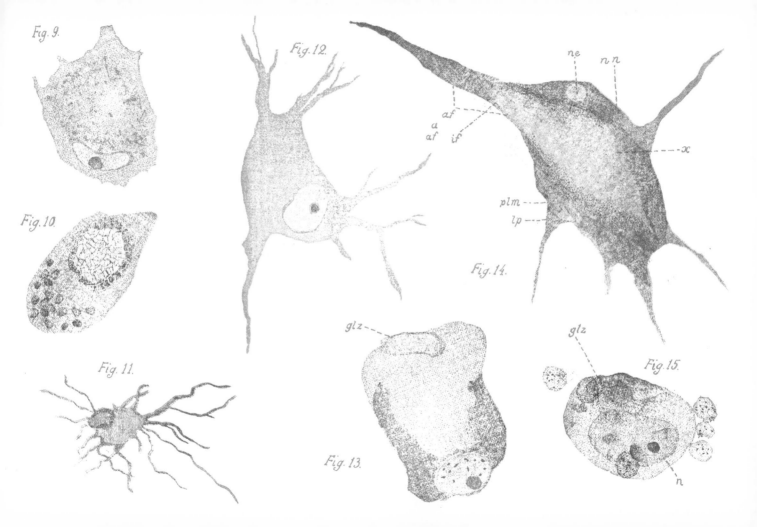

Fig. 9.

Fig. 10.

Fig. 11.

Fig. 12.

Fig. 14.

Fig. 13.

Fig. 15.

ne

n n

af

a
af

if

x

plm

lp

glz

glz

n